W9-BSK-963

Dear Reader—

In every interaction with our children, we are reminded that they are filled with possibilities. Each conversation we share is a window into their potential, and it is our job as their parents to guide them along their own unique paths toward achievement. These moments together shape their growth and renew our belief in the promise that every child holds.

Not every child, however, has this special relationship with a caring adult—even though we know that such early connections foster the social, emotional, and early literacy skills that children need to succeed in school and in life. While overwhelming research shows that quality early learning experiences are a way out of poverty, a path toward a future full of opportunity, and a known deterrent to crime and drug use, more than one-third of America's young children will *still* enter kindergarten this year without the reading or language skills necessary to succeed at grade level. When we learned about Jumpstart's efforts to address this problem, we decided to act.

Please join us in taking action to advance the potential of every child through Jumpstart's Read for the Record campaign.

Through this campaign, Jumpstart is directly educating families about the benefits of reading with children and supporting the vital work of preparing every child for school success.

Last year more than 150,000 children read Jumpstart's Read for the Record official campaign book with an adult, and together we set a new world record. This year, we hope to see that record broken as we read *The Story of Ferdinand*. Children will be thrilled to meet Ferdinand, a simple hero who breaks free from the expectations of those around him to forge his own path.

By participating in the campaign, you will help raise awareness of the importance of early education, strengthen a connection with a young child in your life, and help expand Jumpstart's early education programs that connect at-risk preschool children with trained, caring mentors.

We invite you to share this inspiring book and help children achieve their potential. Please Read for the Record—for yourself, for your family and community, and for the children Jumpstart will reach across America.

Sincerely,

Matt Lauer   Meredith Vieira

i

THE STORY OF JUMPSTART

Thank you for purchasing this custom limited edition of *The Story of Ferdinand* and for participating in Jumpstart's Read for the Record. At Jumpstart, we believe every child enters the world with potential and deserves the resources and support necessary to succeed in school and in life.

For the Record . . . Too Many Children Enter School Unprepared to Learn

In the United States today, as many as 35 percent of children enter our schools without the skills needed to succeed.[1] In our nation's low-income communities children receive as few as 25 hours of one-to-one reading by age 5, while their middle-income peers have been read to as many as 1,700 hours by the same age.[2] Those children receiving fewer hours of reading are likely to enter kindergarten with one-fourth the vocabulary of their mid-income peers.[3]

For the Record . . . Jumpstart Helps Children Thrive

Jumpstart is a national nonprofit organization that has been working within low-income communities since 1993 to prepare preschoolers for kindergarten—one child at a time. At 70 colleges throughout the United States, 3,000 college students work one-to-one with Jumpstart children, who are at risk of entering kindergarten behind their peers. Together these dedicated college students are serving 12,000 preschool children in communities across the country.

For the Record . . . You Can Help

Last year more than 150,000 children across the country participated in Jumpstart's Read for the Record campaign by reading the same book with an adult on one record-setting day in libraries, classrooms, homes, stores, and parent groups. We need your help to connect even more children and adults in the powerful learning relationships that model Jumpstart's work in classrooms every day.

Just by purchasing this book you will be supporting Jumpstart's work in low-income communities, as 100 percent of the proceeds fund our work with at-risk children.

Get Involved in Jumpstart

1 **Read:** Pledge to read with a child in your life; Jumpstart receives $1 from Hanna Andersson for every registrant.

2 **Connect:** Celebrate Jumpstart's Read for the Record in your community. Join or build a local reading event.

3 **Support:** Donate Jumpstart's custom limited edition of *The Story of Ferdinand* to a child in need.

Visit www.readfortherecord.org to participate and learn more.

---

1. Landry, S. 2005. Chapter 6: Content areas. *Effective early childhood programs: Turning knowledge into action.*

2. McQuillan, J. 1998. *The literacy crisis: False claims, real solutions.*

3. Hart, B. and T. R. Risley. 1995. *Meaningful differences in the everyday experience of young American children.*

MAKE THE MOST OF READING TOGETHER

"Oral language is the foundation for literacy development. Oral language provides children with a sense of words and sentences . . . [T]hrough their own speech children demonstrate their understanding of the meanings of words and written materials." [4]

The following tips are based on proven reading techniques developed through expert research and adapted by Jumpstart. Reading with your child on a regular basis is very important, and simple techniques like the ones listed below can increase the quality of the learning experience.

Begin Early and Read Often

The journey begins at birth. Years of playing, talking, listening, and reading together become the foundation for literacy skills, social development, and success in classrooms and in life.
Reading with your child every day is a wonderful way to:

- Increase your child's knowledge about people, places, and things.
- Help your child learn the meaning of new words, letters, and sounds.
- Give your child an opportunity to practice speaking and listening.
- Encourage lifelong, positive attitudes toward reading.

Make Reading a Conversation

While engaging your child in a conversation about this or any book, your goal is to have the child become the teller of the story.

- Take turns retelling and recalling story events.
- Have a discussion in which you both ask and respond to questions.
- Listen to find out more about your child's knowledge and interests as they relate to the book.
- Share and highlight new words and their meanings.
- Reread the book to deepen your child's understanding of words and concepts.
- Ask your child one or two questions per page that begin with the words *what, where, when, why,* and *how* . . . and wait for a response.
- Make sound effects, and read with expression and enthusiasm.

And remember, the conversations you have before, during, and after reading are just as important as the actual reading. Have fun!

Build Language through Reading

Recent research suggests that a rich vocabulary is a vital platform for early reading. *The Story of Ferdinand*, like many books, is filled with new words that can help children along the path to literacy.

Here are some new vocabulary words, along with simple, child-friendly definitions.

- **Spain** is a country in Europe where bullfights are popular.
- A **bull** is a male cow. Bulls are often very large and strong.
- Feeling **lonesome** means feeling sad because you are all by yourself and you would rather be with a friend.
- A **matador** is the most skillful bullfighter and the last person to fight the bull.
- A **bull ring** is a place where people come to watch bullfights; it's similar to a stadium.

---

4. Ranweiler, L. W. 2004. *Preschool readers and writers: Early literacy strategies for teachers.*

MAKING CONNECTIONS ... CREATING MEANING

Reading *The Story of Ferdinand* together offers a wonderful opportunity to use conversation to introduce some new words and meanings to your child.

Pairing new vocabulary with illustrations and a child's own experiences can provoke great conversations. Here are some examples:

Sting (p. 36)

- As you finish reading the words on the page, explain what the word "sting" means. You might say, "*A sting is like a sharp poke—what a pin feels like—and it really hurts for a moment, then it feels better.*"

- Follow up with a question to connect the child to his or her own experience with being stung. If the child can't think of an example, share one yourself.

- Next look at the picture and talk about Ferdinand's expression. Ask the child, "*What do you think Ferdinand's face is telling us?*"

Scared Stiff (p. 58)

- When you read the words "scared stiff," use your voice and body to express the meaning of these words.

- Explain the meaning of each word by saying something like, "*Scared stiff means you are so surprised and frightened that your body tightens up. It gets straight and still—you don't move.*"

- Invite the child to join you in imitating the expression and see how "scared stiff" you and your child can get.

- Ask the child to share a story about when he or she was so frightened, (s)he was "scared stiff."

After you read the entire story, return to these pages (and others) to revisit the new words and their meanings. Ask a simple question like, "*Why do you think the Matador was scared stiff?*" These kinds of discussions will show you if the child understands and can recall the meaning of the words.

Please visit us online at www.readfortherecord.org for more tips on effective reading with a young child.

BE TRUE TO YOURSELF!

In this picture Ferdinand is doing what he wants to do, even though people really want him to fight the bullfighters. Ferdinand is more interested in smelling the flowers in the lovely ladies' hair than he is in fighting.

What Do You Like to Do?

As a way to extend the learning from *The Story of Ferdinand*, we invite you to talk with a child in your life about something that he or she loves to do. It's not important if others enjoy this activity, it's only important that the child enjoys it, just like Ferdinand loved sitting quietly smelling the flowers.

We hope this will lead to a whole new conversation between you and a young child in your life about his or her dreams for the future.

Please visit www.readfortherecord.org/shareyourstory to share your child's story and to read inspiring stories from around the world!

READ FOR THE RECORD
jumpstart

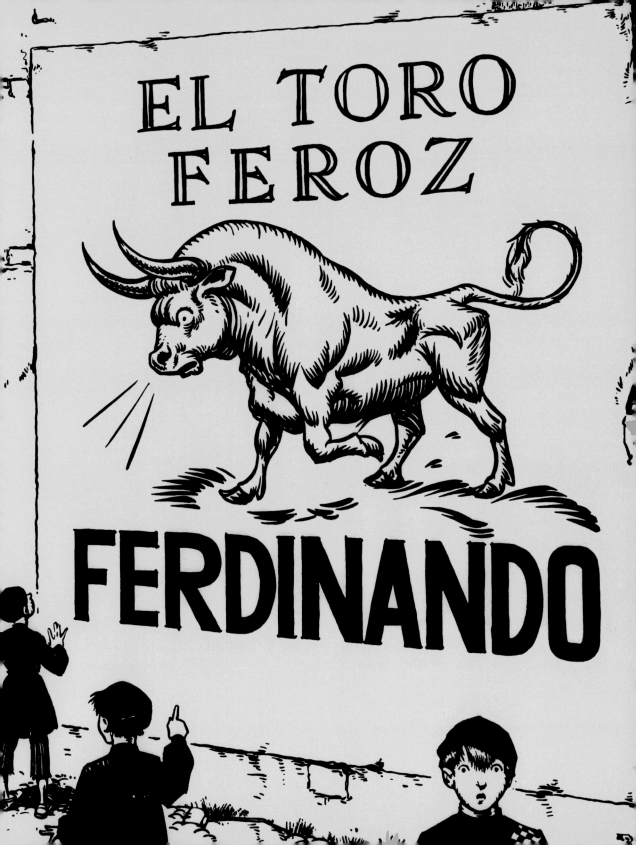

The Story of
FERDINAND

By Munro Leaf

Illustrated by Robert Lawson

VIKING

VIKING

Published by Penguin Group

Penguin Young Readers Group, 345 Hudson Street, New York, New York 10014, U.S.A.

Penguin Group (Canada), 90 Eglinton Avenue East, Suite 700, Toronto, Ontario, Canada M4P 2Y3

(a division of Pearson Penguin Canada Inc.)

Penguin Books Ltd, 80 Strand, London WC2R 0RL, England

Penguin Ireland, 25 St Stephen's Green, Dublin 2, Ireland (a division of Penguin Books Ltd)

Penguin Group (Australia), 250 Camberwell Road, Camberwell, Victoria 3124, Australia

(a division of Pearson Australia Group Pty Ltd)

Penguin Books India Pvt Ltd, 11 Community Centre, Panchsheel Park, New Delhi – 110 017, India

Penguin Group (NZ), 67 Apollo Drive, Mairangi Bay, Auckland 1311, New Zealand

(a division of Pearson New Zealand Ltd.)

Penguin Books (South Africa) (Pty) Ltd, 24 Sturdee Avenue, Rosebank, Johannesburg 2196, South Africa

Penguin Books Ltd, Registered Offices: 80 Strand, London WC2R 0RL, England

First published in 1936 by The Viking Press

This special edition published in 2007 by Viking, a division of Penguin Young Readers Group

1 3 5 7 9 10 8 6 4 2

The Library of Congress has cataloged the previous edition under catalog card number: 36-19452   Pic Bk

ISBN 978-0-670-67424-4

This edition ISBN 978-0-670-06264-5

Manufactured in China

Once upon a time in Spain

there was a little bull and his name was Ferdinand.

All the other little bulls he lived with would run and jump and butt their heads together,

but not Ferdinand.

He liked to sit just quietly and smell the flowers.

He had a favorite spot out in
the pasture under a cork tree.

It was his favorite tree and he would sit in its shade all day and smell the flowers.

Sometimes his mother, who was a cow, would worry about him. She was afraid he would be lonesome all by himself.

"Why don't you run and play with the other little bulls and skip and butt your head?" she would say.

But Ferdinand would shake his head. "I like it better here where I can sit just quietly and smell the flowers."

His mother saw that he was not lonesome, and because she was an understanding mother, even though she was a cow, she let him just sit there and be happy.

As the years went by Ferdinand grew and grew until he was very big and strong.

FERDINAND
2 years

FERDINAND
1 year

3 MONTHS

1 week

RL

All the other bulls who had grown up with him in the same pasture would fight each other all day. They would butt each other and stick each other with their horns. What they wanted most of all was to be picked to fight at the bull fights in Madrid.

But not Ferdinand—he still liked to sit just quietly under the cork tree and smell the flowers.

One day five men came in very funny hats to pick the biggest, fastest, roughest bull to fight in the bull fights in Madrid.

All the other bulls ran around snorting and butting, leaping and jumping so the men would think that they were very very strong and fierce and pick them.

Ferdinand knew that they wouldn't pick him and he didn't care. So he went out to his favorite cork tree to sit down.

RL

He didn't look where he was sitting and instead of sitting on the nice cool grass in the shade he sat on a bumble bee.

Well, if you were a bumble bee and a bull sat on you what would you do? You would sting him. And that is just what this bee did to Ferdinand.

Wow! Did it hurt! Ferdinand jumped up with a snort. He ran around puffing and snorting, butting and pawing the ground as if he were crazy.

The five men saw him and they all shouted with joy. Here was the largest and fiercest bull of all. Just the one for the bull fights in Madrid!

So they took him away for the
bull fight day in a cart.

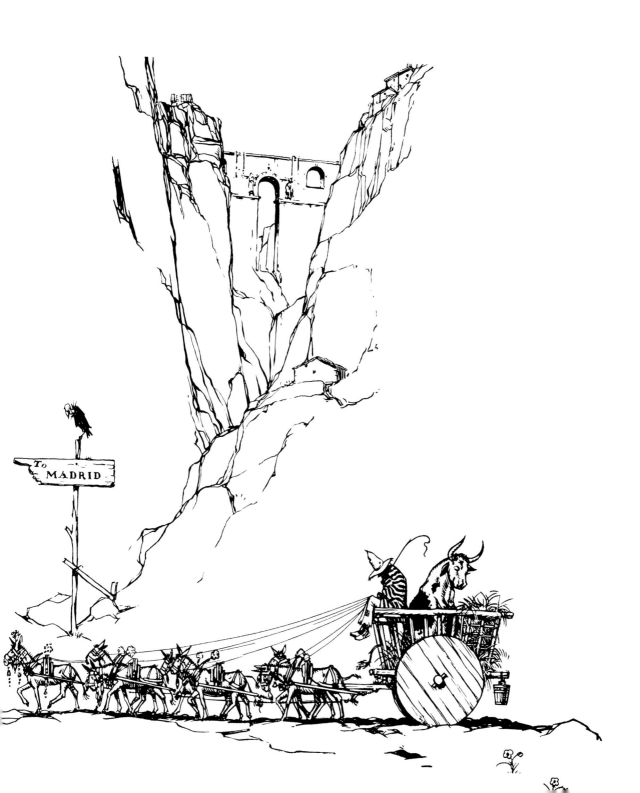

What a day it was! Flags were
flying, bands were playing . . .

and all the lovely ladies had
flowers in their hair.

GALERÍA

FERDINANDO

FERDINANDO

FERDINANDO

NANDO
O TORO

They had a parade into the
bull ring.

49

First came the Banderilleros
with long sharp pins with
ribbons on them to stick in
the bull and make him mad.

Next came the Picadores who rode skinny horses and they had long spears to stick in the bull and make him madder.

Then came the Matador, the proudest of all—he thought he was very handsome, and bowed to the ladies. He had a red cape and a sword and was supposed to stick the bull last of all.

Then came the bull, and you know who that was don't you?

—FERDINAND.

They called him Ferdinand the Fierce and all the Banderilleros were afraid of him and the Picadores were afraid of him and the Matador was scared stiff.

Ferdinand ran to the middle of the ring and everyone shout-ed and clapped because they thought he was going to fight fiercely and butt and snort and stick his horns around.

But not Ferdinand. When he got to the middle of the ring he saw the flowers in all the lovely ladies' hair and he just sat down quietly and smelled.

He wouldn't fight and be fierce no matter what they did. He just sat and smelled. And the Banderilleros were mad and the Picadores were madder and the Matador was so mad he cried because he couldn't show off with his cape and sword.

So they had to take Ferdinand home.

And for all I know he is sitting there still, under his favorite cork tree, smelling the flowers just quietly.

He is very happy.

THE END